The Wiggle Wobble Story

Duane N. Maas

Illustrated by Steve and James Stone

Stories with a Point

He drove the tractor up to the house, got off, and ran inside. He said, "Ma, Ma, there are some monsters over in the pasture and they have

> *six eyes,*
> *four noses,*
> *twelve ears,*
> *a great big mouth* and
> *warts as big as your hand!*"

She said, "You're kidding!?"

He said, "No, and they were rolling down the green grassy hillside going *lblblblblblblbl.*"

She said, "Oh, I feel terrible! A few weeks ago the children said they saw something like that and I didn't believe them. Oh, I feel terrible, what if they had harmed the children?"

They got on the phone and called several of the neighbors to see if they had seen the monsters. No one had, but they all agreed that anything that looked that awful must be bad and they should get rid of them.

Well, time went by. One day the father was out mowing hay and he looked over toward the pasture. He saw the wiggle wobbles rolling down the green grassy hillside. He said, "Look at those monsters! They have

six eyes,
four noses,
twelve ears,
a great big mouth and
warts as big as your hand!"

The mother said, "Oh you children have such an imagination."

They said, "No we really saw them and they were rolling down the green grassy hillside going **blblblblblblblbl**."

She said, "I don't want to hear any more about it. It's time for supper, so please go get washed up."

The children ran home, burst through the screen door, and ran into the kitchen. They said, "Mama, Mama, we saw some monsters that had

six eyes,

four noses,

twelve ears,

a great big mouth and

warts as big as your hand!"

Well, time went by. One day the children were out playing hide and go seek. Tommy was it and he was counting,

one, two, three, four, five, six..."

Little Sara was looking for a place to hide when she saw the bucket on the old well. Now, mother had always said, 'don't go near the old well.' Sara thought, 'I won't get hurt.' So she climbed up into the bucket. The bucket and Sara fell into the well. Sara stuck in the mud on the bottom. She was not really hurt, but she was afraid and she was crying.

Finally the other children heard her, but they could not get her out.

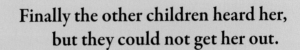

People would walk by saying,
'Look at that monster! He has
   six eyes,
   four noses,
   twelve ears,
   a great big mouth and
   warts as big as your hand!'

They would laugh, poke fun at
him and throw their bubble gum
at him. The bubble gum would
stick to his soft skin. The wiggle
wobble did not laugh any more.
Instead he cried,
   *Wa... wa... wa... wa.**

*Children are to imitate crying like a wiggle wobble.

Then one day, after a shower of rain, the sun came out. One of the wiggle wobbles looked out of the hole and saw the bright sunshine on the green grassy hillside and said, "I can't resist!" The others tried to stop him, but he went any way. He was rolling down the green grassy hillside going *blblblblblblblbl*.

The people saw him and they snuck up on the wiggle wobble. They threw a net over him and put him in a cage in the zoo.

The people organized a wiggle wobble hunt. They got out their fish nets, ball bats, and pitch forks and went hunting the wiggle wobbles. They didn't find any wiggle wobbles so they thought, 'maybe they usually only come out at night.' So, they set their alarm clocks for midnight and until four in the morning they took their coon dogs, flash lights, ball bats and fish nets looking for wiggle wobbles. But they still did not find them.

The wiggle wobbles were hiding in their hole in the ground and had put a rock over the top so no one could find them.

One day the wiggle wobbles were rolling down the green grassy hillside and they rolled right past some children who were playing. The children screamed,

"Eakkkk!
 Look at those monsters!
They have
> *six eyes,*
> *four noses,*
> *twelve ears,*
> *a great big mouth* and
> *warts as big as your hand!*
> *Awhhhh!"*

Once upon a time, there were three wiggle wobbles. Wiggle wobbles are big and heavy, and soft and smooth. They have

six eyes,
four noses,
twelve ears,
a great big mouth and
warts as big as your hand!

Wiggle wobbles love to roll down the green grassy hillside on bright sunny days. The grass tickles their soft skin and they laugh, *blblblblblblblbl.**

*Encourage children to imitate and repeat this sound each time in the story.

They went and got their parents, but they could not get her out. People were anxious and mothers were crying when the two wiggle wobbles heard the commotion. They had a tunnel from their hole into the old well because that is where they used to get their drinking water. When the two wiggle wobbles got to the old well they said, "why look, it's little Sara. She seems trapped, maybe we can help!" The wiggle wobbles got into the well by little Sara.

Sara's father looked down the well and saw the two wiggle wobbles. He cried out, Eakkk, look at those monsters! They have

six eyes,
four noses,
twelve ears,
a great big mouth and
warts as big as your hand!

They are going to eat my little Sara and we can't stop them! I can't look!"

But the wiggle wobbles did not eat little Sara. Instead they got under her and pushed her up to the top. She jumped into her father's arms and was safe.

Then the people realized that the wiggle wobbles were not that bad after all. They said, "They saved little Sara!"

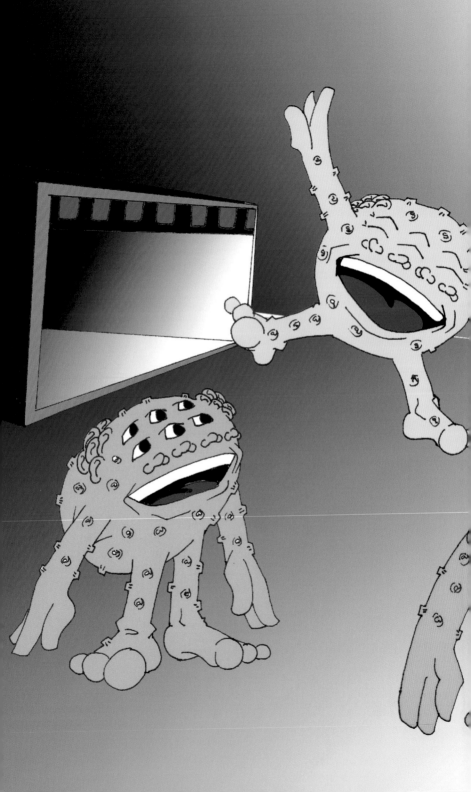

Then the people were
sorry they had caught
the wiggle wobble and
had put him in the zoo.
So, they took the wiggle
wobble out of the cage,
washed off all the bubble
gum from his soft skin and
set him free!

From then on the children and the wiggle wobbles were allowed to play together. The wiggle wobbles would roll down the green grassy hillside and laugh, *blblblblblblbl*. Then the children would tickle them with long blades of grass and the wiggle wobbles would laugh some more. *Blblblblblbblbl*.

Welcome to the yearly
Wiggle Wobble
festival

Each year they would have a wiggle wobble festival. The wiggle wobbles would be the guests of honor. There was a parade and the wiggle wobbles would ride in the back of a convertible, smiling and waving to the people. They would have games and contests such as who could roll down the green grassy hillside the fastest, who could laugh the most like a wiggle wobble, and who could grow the biggest warts!

The End

The Wiggle Wobble Story
Copyright ©2008 Duane N. Maas
All rights reserved

Cover Design by Pine Hill Graphics
Interior Design by Pine Hill Graphics

This story teaches us to not judge people by appearance.
It is a book helping against prejudice and promoting acceptance and love.
Biblical Teaching: Col. 3:12-16, 1 Cor. 12:12-27; Eph. 2:13-14

Publisher's Cataloging-in-Publication Data
(Provided by Cassidy Cataloguing Services, Inc.)

Maas, Duane N.

    The wiggle wobble story / Duane N. Maas ; illustrated by Steve and
James Stone. -- 1st ed. -- Springfield, MO : Stories with a Point,
2008.

       p. ; cm.
       ISBN: 978-1-933150-15-4
       Summary: The Wiggle Wobble Story is a charming tale that
reminds us to not judge by appearances. It is a story to help fight
against prejudice by promoting acceptance and love.

      1. Toleration--Juvenile fiction. 2. Prejudices--Juvenile fiction.
3. Values--Juvenile fiction. 4. Individuality--Juvenile fiction.
I. Stone, Steve. II. Stone, James. III. Title.

HM1271 .M33 2008
303.385--dc22   0801

Printed in the United States of America.